PUFFIN BOOKS

Aussie Bites

The Sugar-Gum Tree

Sarah Bell and Penny May
were best friends. Sometimes they
had fights, but after the fights
they were best friends again.

Then one day they had
a very bad fight.

Which Aussie Bites have you read?

Aussie Bites

The Sugar-Gum Tree

Patricia Wrightson

Illustrated by David Cox

Puffin Books

Puffin Books
Penguin Books Australia Ltd
487 Maroondah Highway, PO Box 257
Ringwood, Victoria 3134, Australia
Penguin Books Ltd
Harmondsworth, Middlesex, England
Penguin Putnam Inc.
375 Hudson Street, New York, New York 10014, USA
Penguin Books Canada Limited
10 Alcorn Avenue, Toronto, Ontario, Canada, M4V 3B2
Penguin Books (N.Z.) Ltd
Cnr Rosedale and Airborne Roads, Albany, Auckland, New Zealand
Penguin Books (South Africa) (Pty) Ltd
5 Watkins Street, Denver Ext 4, 2094, South Africa
Penguin Books India (P) Ltd
11, Community Centre, Panchsheel Park, New Delhi – 110 017, India

First published in Viking by Penguin Books Australia, 1991
First published in Puffin, 1993
This edition first published, 1999

1 3 5 7 9 10 8 6 4 2

Typeset in New Century Schoolbook
by Post Pre-press Group, Brisbane
Made and printed in Australia by Australian Print Group,
Maryborough, Victoria

Designed by Nikki Townsend, Penguin Design Studio
Series designed by Ruth Grüner
Series editor: Kay Ronai
Front cover illustration coloured by Terry Denton

National Library of Australia
Cataloguing-in-Publication data:
Wrightson, Patricia, 1921– .
The sugar-gum tree.
ISBN 0 14 130691 2.
I. Cox, David, 1933– . II. Title. (Series: Aussie bites).
A823.3

www.puffin.com.au

One

Sarah Bell and Penny May were
best friends. They both played in
the Bells' yard, or they both played
in the Mays' yard.

Sometimes they had fights.
Then Sarah talked and smiled in a
grown-up way. It made Penny mad.
If she stomped about and shouted
a bit, the fight was soon over; but

if Penny had a red face and tight-shut lips, it was a bad fight.

After the fights they were best friends again.

Sarah was making a house,

under the sugar-gum tree in her
back yard. Penny came round
to help. There was a lot of stuff
lying around the tree. Penny
had a good look.

'Where did the rug come from?' she asked.

'The tip,' Sarah told her. 'When Dad took me. It's clean, even. Mum helped me.'

'It's magic. What are the bricks
for?'

'The stove, I think. Or it could
be chairs.'

'There's a lot. You can have

a little stove and two chairs.'

Sarah frowned; she hadn't made up her mind. She said, 'The stove has to fit the pan Mum gave me.'

Penny went to look at the pan. 'Cups too!' she cried. 'Your mother gave you cups!'

'Only two,' said Sarah. 'And they're cracked.'

'I was going to bring my old teaset!'

'You still can,' said Sarah

quickly, because she could tell
that Penny was hurt. 'We need
more cups and there's no
teapot.'

'You know my teapot's broken,'
Penny said in a grumpy way.

She *was* hurt.

The house was made from
an old quilt. Sarah tied it to
the tree with string.

'That needs a nail,' said
Penny. She was good with nails.
She went into Mr Bell's shed

and came back with a hammer
and a nail.

'Oh, Penny!' cried Sarah. 'You
can't put a nail in Dad's good
sugar-gum tree.' Sarah was good
with string, and it was her house.

'If a wind comes,' said Penny,
'the whole house could blow
away.' She stood on an apple-
crate and nailed the quilt to
the tree.

'Now you've made the house
crooked,' Sarah told her crossly.

Penny reached up to pull the quilt straight. There was a loud, cracking noise, and she tumbled down. The thin wood of the apple-crate had broken.

'Look what you've done!' cried Sarah. 'That was my table! Penny May, you're a gloop!'

Penny stood up slowly. She was frowning, and there was a long, red scratch on her leg. She said, 'That's not very nice. Calling people a . . .'

'A gloop,' said Sarah, helping in a grown-up way.

'. . . when they've fallen down and hurt their leg and they're only trying to help. You ought to say sorry.'

'Me?' said Sarah, smiling her

grown-up smile. '*You* ought to say sorry. Putting nails into Dad's tree and breaking my table. Go on. Say you're sorry.'

Penny shut her lips tight. Her face went red. She jumped at a branch of the sugar-gum tree,

pulled herself up and began

to climb.

'Come down!' Sarah called, but

Penny went on climbing. 'You're

only being another gloop!' cried
Sarah.

Penny climbed quite high.
Then she sat in the fork of
a branch and shouted angrily,
'I won't come down till you say
you're sorry!'

Two

Sarah was upset; but of course she wasn't sorry. It was her house, and people should make their house their own way. It wasn't fair for Sarah to say sorry when Penny was the one to blame. But when would Penny come down from the tree?

Sarah didn't know what to do,

so she went on making the house. Penny went on sitting in the tree. She didn't even look down, but stared away over all the back yards.

Sarah put the old rug into

the house for a floor. She carried

bricks in, and made a stove and

two chairs. She turned the apple-

crate over to hide the broken

part, and put it in the place for

a table. She put the cups on the

table and the pan on the stove.

Penny was still sitting in
the tree.

'I think that looks nice,' said
Sarah. She said it to herself, but
loudly, in case Penny wanted to
come down and look. 'But there
ought to be flowers.' She went to
the geraniums under her bedroom
window, and picked some flowers.
She put them in a cup on the table.

Penny stared away at the
back yards.

'It's nearly dinner-time,' said Sarah, to herself but loudly. 'Dad will be home soon.' She waited for a bit, but nothing happened.

This was a very bad fight, and Penny was stuck in it.

Sarah went slowly across the yard to the proper house. She thought maybe her mother could sort things out.

Mrs Bell was in the kitchen. She said, 'You're in early. Has Penny gone home?'

'No,' said Sarah, not looking

at anything.

'Where is she, then?'

'In the sugar-gum tree,' said Sarah.

Mrs Bell dropped a potato. 'Sarah, that tree isn't safe. You've both been told that the branches often break.'

'I know,' said Sarah. 'She won't come down.'

'Oh, Sarah, not another fight!' Mrs Bell dried her hands. 'You come with me, young lady.' She marched out to the sugar-gum tree, with Sarah trailing behind.

'Penny!' called Mrs Bell. 'Be careful of that tree, dear! Its branches break quite easily. You'd better come down now, anyway. It's nearly dinner-time.'

Penny's face got red again. 'Sarah's got to say sorry. She called me a . . .'

'A gloop,' said Sarah in a small voice.

'She's got to say sorry,' called Penny, hugging the tree's trunk in case the branch broke.

'SARAH,' said Mrs Bell sternly.

'I'm sorry,' whispered Sarah, though she knew it wasn't fair.

'Say it louder. She's right up the tree.'

Sarah put her head back and
shouted, 'I'M SORRY!' Then she

added, just moving her lips and
making no sound, 'That Penny
May is such a gloop.'

'She said it again!' shouted Penny. 'I saw her! She called me it again!'

'Sarah,' said Mrs Bell, 'go to your room and stay there. Penny May, I'm going to ring up your mother. She'll be home from work by now.'

Sarah slumped off to her bedroom.

Three

Sarah flopped down on her bed. She could hear Mrs Bell ringing up Mrs May. Sitting on the bed, she stared glumly out of her window. There was the quilt-house, still a bit crooked. There was Penny, so high in the sugar-gum tree that she looked small. Now her face wasn't red; it was

glum, like Sarah's, and she clung

tight to the tree.

Sarah gave her a little wave;

they were both in the same

trouble. And it must be bad for

Penny, high up in the Bells' tree
with her mother coming.

The car drove into the shed:
now Dad was home. He came into
the yard, and stopped to look at
the quilt-house, shaking his head.

He picked up his hammer and
put it away. Then he went inside.
He hadn't looked up into the tree.

Sarah waited. Mum and Dad
were talking in the kitchen. After
a while, Dad came out again.

'Hi, there!' he called into the sugar-gum. 'Are you going to stay and have dinner with Sarah?'

Penny shook her head. Her mouth was tight shut. Sarah saw that Penny couldn't talk now, even if she tried.

'It's not very nice,' called Mr Bell, 'spending the night in a tree. What if you go to sleep? Will you fall?'

Penny looked as if she might cry.

'Don't you want to get down before your mother comes?' called Mr Bell. 'We can all have a Coke while we wait.'

Penny shook her head again. Mr Bell came over to look at the geraniums. Then he looked through the window, at Sarah.

'You know you're a brat, don't you?' he said in a cross voice. 'It's time you got some sense.'

It wasn't fair, but Sarah didn't
tell him; now she couldn't talk,
either. She only looked at him,
and he went inside.

The front door-bell rang, and

the house was full of voices: both
Mr and Mrs May had come. There
was loud talking for a while, and
suddenly all the grown-ups spilt
out of the back door into the yard.

'Penny!' cried Mrs May. 'You come
down out of that tree this very
minute, do you hear?'

'And stay close to the trunk!'
called Mr May.

Penny stared at all the people.
Then she screwed up her mouth
and shut her eyes.

Mrs Bell called to her, coaxing.

'Penny, dear, I promise nobody is

going to be cross. Just come down

while it's still daylight, and before

you fall. Sarah is going to say

she's sorry.'

Penny clung to the tree and

stared away over all the back yards.

'I know what it is,' said Mrs May.

'The child is badly frightened.

Penny, dear, can you hear me?

Don't be scared, we're all here to

help. Just come down a little bit,

if you can; just one branch for now.'

Penny shut her eyes and

scrunched herself tighter to the tree.

'If you can't, never mind,' called

Mrs May quickly. 'Just hang on
and keep still. Dad will call the
Fire Brigade.'

Sarah gasped. The Fire
Brigade! Oh, no!

'NO!' shouted Penny furiously,
and shut her mouth tight. Her
face was very red.

Sarah felt sick with worry.

'For goodness sake!' called Mrs
May. 'What are we to do, then?
You know we can't leave you in
a tree all night.'

Penny kept her mouth shut.
For a minute the grown-ups
talked softly to each other. Then
Mr May went inside to call the
Fire Brigade. All the grown-ups
stood gazing into the tree.

Soon, from a long way off, came
the howling of a siren.

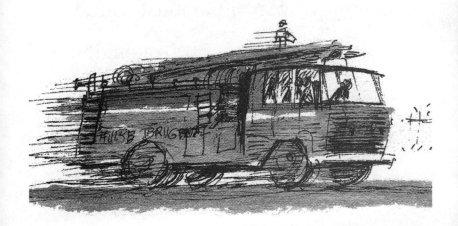

Four

The siren came nearer. Penny
wound her arms and legs harder
round the tree. Sarah felt dreadful.

The wailing noise came nearer,
nearer; it was the loudest sound
in the world. The red fire-engine
rushed howling round the corner.
It stopped outside the Bells'
back fence.

There were four firemen. They
talked in loud, kind voices to the
grown-ups and to Penny. They put

up a ladder, right over the
back fence and into the sugar-
gum tree.

One man came climbing along
the ladder. He kept talking

loudly and kindly to Penny. He

told her it was all right, she was

quite safe, he was coming; and

he told her he had a little

girl of his own, about her size.

Penny kept her eyes and
mouth tight shut. She gripped
the tree with her arms and
legs and clung like a koala. The
fireman couldn't pull her off.

'That's a good, sensible girl,' he said, 'holding on so tight. But I've got you safe; you can let go now.'

Penny didn't let go. She clung like a koala. The fireman talked and pulled for a long time. At last he gave in, and went back along the ladder. He told Mr May he was afraid of breaking the tree.

Everyone was worried. Mrs May was crying. All the firemen talked to Mr May and Mr Bell. They said something about a net.

'What for?' said Penny's fireman. 'She's not going to fall.'

The men took the ladder down, and Mr Bell herded everyone into the house.

They went on talking in a
worried way. It was beginning to
get dark.

Sarah pushed her window
wide open. She put her chair
near it, climbed over the sill,

 jumped down
into the
geraniums,
and ran very
fast to the
sugar-
gum tree.

'Quick, Penny!' she shouted.

'Now! This way, quick!'

Penny came climbing and
tumbling out of the tree.

Five

Penny reached the lowest branch and fell on to Sarah. They scrambled up and ran to the window. The sill was high, but they jumped and wriggled and pulled themselves up. They had to.

At last they were standing in Sarah's room, staring at each other. They still couldn't believe it.

The Fire Brigade!

'What now?' said Penny in
a tight, hard voice.

Sarah didn't know what now, but
she knew it had to be fast or her
mother would be here. She said,
'We'll just get into bed, and serve

them right. Here – pyjamas –

hurry up! Mum's sure to come.'

Quickly they put on pyjamas

and climbed into Sarah's bed.

There were footsteps coming

down the hall. Sarah and Penny lay down and shut their eyes. They had just fitted themselves together when the door opened, and Mrs Bell switched on the light.

She didn't say a word. She just looked for a while and went away.

Sarah and Penny stayed as they were. They didn't know what else to do.

Then there were loud, grown-up voices saying things like *'What?'* and *'Never!'* and *'Can't be!'*

Someone – it might have been
Penny's fireman – said, '*Well, I'll
be a monkey's uncle!*' A lot of feet
came shuffling down the hall.

Sarah and Penny lay still. They could tell that all the people were crowding in the doorway, looking at them.

'Kids,' said a fireman. 'Can't beat 'em, can you?'

'I might,' said Mr Bell, but he didn't sound cross. He sounded very tired.

'I owe you chaps something for your trouble,' said Mr May. He sounded tired too. The firemen made soft, rumbling noises, and shuffled away down the hall after Mr May.

Sarah and Penny opened their eyes. Mr and Mrs Bell and Mrs May were still there. They all looked tired.

'Penny's staying the night,' said Sarah. 'Aren't you, Penny?'

'Umph,' grunted Penny. She

still couldn't talk much.

'Is she?' said Mrs Bell.

'I thought you'd had a fight.'

'It couldn't be helped,' said Sarah. 'It was *our* fight.'

'Fair enough,' said Mr Bell, 'and it's *our* sugar-gum tree. And the next person who climbs it is going to get well and truly spanked.'

'Twice,' added Mrs May.

'Three times,' said Mr May coming back.

'That's fair enough too,' said Mrs Bell, 'but I promised Penny no one would be cross if she came down. Do you think this time we might just feed them and shut them up in Sarah's room till morning?'

'Well . . .' said Mrs and Mr May, thinking it over.

Sarah and Penny stayed in bed. It seemed safest, and they were tired too.

Six

In the end, Mr and Mrs May
went home and Penny stayed
with Sarah. They were still in bed,
and Mrs Bell brought them dinner
on a tray. It was hard to manage,
with two people in one bed.

'You're tipping it up!' cried
Sarah when Penny moved
her legs.

'Stop knocking my elbow, Sarah,'
growled Penny.

Later, when the light was out,
they lay fitted together and
thought about things. Sarah was
nearly asleep when Penny jerked
a bit and woke her up.

'Do you have to joggle?' said

Sarah, sleepy. 'What's up?'

'The . . . the Fire Brigade!'

whispered Penny, and pulled
the blanket over her head and
shook with giggles.

Sarah was surprised and
glad, so she started giggling too.
'I'll be a monkey's uncle!' she
whispered, and they giggled
about that. They went on
giggling till they fell asleep.

Seven

In the morning, after breakfast,
Penny went home. Sarah went
with her to the gate.

'I'll bring my teaset,' said
Penny.

'Good,' said Sarah. She climbed
on the gate to watch Penny walk
away down the pavement.

When Penny was nearly at the

corner, Sarah leaned out from

the gate and shouted, 'Penny!'

Penny stopped and turned back.

'I'm sorry . . .'

'Oh, no!' cried Penny, and

started to run.

'. . . THAT PENNY MAY IS SUCH A GLOOP!' shouted Sarah as fast as she could.

But Penny had turned the corner just in time.

From Patricia Wrightson

I wrote *The Sugar-Gum Tree* a long time ago
as a picture book, but it wasn't right for the
big, colourful kind. I put it away.

Much later I met David Cox. He read the story,
liked it, and wanted to illustrate it, so we
talked to Puffin. That was the first time David
and I worked together, and since then he has
worked on all my *Aussie Bites*. We seem to like
the same lively sort of character.

From David Cox

I like the people in *The Sugar-Gum Tree*.
When the people are so different from one
another, it is easier, somehow, to see them in
my mind. I added just one more, which
is the dog. We do not know his name; he is just
there, always watching. All the arguments
and drama must seem puzzling to him.
Humans are a funny lot, and, come to think
of it, that is what the story is all about.

Peg Leg Meg and her perky parrot are in deep trouble. Can they escape the evil pirate, Maude the Marauder?

Merry dreams of being a ballerina. And nothing is going to stop her . . .

Something is happening down in the dump, but Dinsmore's school principal doesn't want him to know about it . . .

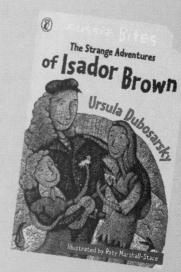

Isador carries six things in his satchel on his travels, one of which is a secret until nearly the end of the story.